For Ciara Rose Thompson with love   **K.S.**

Text by Sophie Piper
Illustrations copyright © 2009 Kristina Stephenson
This edition copyright © 2009 Lion Hudson

The moral rights of the author and illustrator
have been asserted

A Lion Children's Book
an imprint of
Lion Hudson plc
Wilkinson House, Jordan Hill Road,
Oxford OX2 8DR, England
www.lionhudson.com
ISBN: 978 0 7459 6123 1

First edition 2009
1 3 5 7 9 10 8 6 4 2 0

A catalogue record for this book is available
from the British Library

Typeset in 20/26 Baskerville MT Schoolbook
Printed and bound in China

The Angel and the Dove

Sophie Piper

Illustrations by Kristina Stephenson

LION
CHILDREN'S

High in the olive tree, the dove was sitting
on her nest.
   From somewhere among the waving
grasses came the sound of singing.

The dove fluttered down
to look more closely.
There was an angel.
'What are you doing
here?' cooed the dove.

'I'm watching the poppies open,'
replied the angel.
What are you doing?
'Ooh, I have three eggs
in a nest,' replied the dove.
'I must go and keep
them warm.'

And the dove watched as children came into the garden and the angel showed them where new flowers had opened.

The next day, the dove heard the angel humming.

'What are you doing now?' asked the dove.

'I'm watching this newborn butterfly,' said the angel. 'Her wings are only just drying in the sun.'

And all through the morning, the angel danced with the children as they tried to touch the butterflies that flitted among the flowers.

But that afternoon,
a cold wind riffled
through the trees.
The children ran
home.

The angel sat on a stone at the foot
of the olive tree.
'It's sad when friends go away,' she
sighed.
So the dove cooed a gentle
song to try and cheer her.

Then the sun went behind a cloud and the sky went grey.

'It's too cold,' cooed the dove. 'I hope it's not going to be winter again.'

'Spring is meant to be a beginning,' said the angel, 'but today feels like an ending.'

And truly, something sad must have happened that day: for in the evening, the dove heard someone crying.

She saw the angel
bringing her a bunch
of flowers… but even the
flowers were drooping.

Through the next day,
the angel and the dove
sat and watched.

Watched and sat.

Sat and watched.

That night, while it was still dark, the dove
heard the sound she had been waiting for.

A tap-tap-tapping from an egg. Then another.
And another.

She was all in a fluster as her chicks hatched
from their shells.

'Come and see,' she cooed to the angel.

To her surprise, the angel who had been
so sad was dancing.

And so was the woman.

And was that someone else in the garden?

'Everything is alive again!' laughed the angel.
'It's a miracle spring!'
  For truly, it was not just spring, but the very first
Easter.